Watch Me Grow!

Blue Plants a Seed

Blue's Clues®

by Lauryn Silverhardt   illustrated by Karen Craig

Simon Spotlight/Nickelodeon
New York   London   Toronto   Sydney

Based on the TV series *Blue's Clues*® created by Traci Paige Johnson, Todd Kessler, and Angela C. Santomero as seen on Nick Jr.®

SIMON SPOTLIGHT

An imprint of Simon & Schuster Children's Publishing Division

1230 Avenue of the Americas, New York, New York 10020

Manufactured in the United States of America

First Edition 10 9 8 7 6 5 4 3 2 1

ISBN-13: 978-1-4169-6874-0

ISBN-10: 1-4169-6874-1

"It's the first day of spring!" Miss Marigold said to Blue's class. "It's time for us to learn about plants. Who knows what most plants need to grow and stay healthy?"

Magenta raised her hand. "Plants need air, water, and soil," she said.

"Good thinking, Magenta!"
said Miss Marigold. "Plants
also need one more thing. Does
anyone remember? It's bright,
it comes from the sky, and it
makes things warm on a lovely
spring day like today."

Blue knew the answer. "Sunlight!"

"That's right!" Miss Marigold said proudly.

Miss Marigold gave each student a pot to decorate. Then she gave each of them a few seeds. The students filled their pots with rich, fluffy soil and planted their seeds. Then they gently watered the soil.

"Now we will wait until the seeds sprout. Then you can take them home to care for them, and you will see what kind of plants they become!" said Miss Marigold. "When you figure out what kind of plant you have, you can bring it back to school so we can all see it. Then we will plant all of our plants in the school garden for everyone to enjoy."

Over the following weeks, while they waited for the seeds to sprout, Blue and her friends learned all about plants.

"Plants make clean air for us to breathe," reported Periwinkle.

"Some plants make food for us to eat," said Green Puppy.

"Trees make shade to keep us cool on hot, sunny summer days," said Orange Kitten.

"Plants are all around us!" said Blue.

Finally, the seeds sprouted. Blue took her seedling home. She carefully watered the soil and placed the pot on the windowsill, where the seedling would get lots of sunlight.

Each day Blue cared for her seedling. It grew larger slowly, but she still couldn't tell what kind of plant it was.

One day after school Joe, Blue, and Magenta ate a healthy snack of fruits and vegetables.

"We learned in school that fruits and vegetables come from plants," said Magenta. "Do you think our seedlings will make healthy snacks like this?" Blue asked her.

"Mine will!" said Magenta. "I figured out that my seedling is a bean plant. I can tell because of the shape of its leaves."

Blue was happy for Magenta. "I'm excited to see your plant in school tomorrow!" she said. Blue looked at her own plant. She couldn't wait to find out what kind of plant it was.

Magenta and Green Puppy brought their plants to school the next day. Miss Marigold put the plants in the window where all the students could see them.

Over the next few days more students brought their plants in to class. The window was almost full of pots!

Blue wished that her plant was on the window with the others.

The next weekend was sunny and clear. Blue and Joe went outside to see what Shovel and Pail were doing.

"Hi! We're planting lily bulbs," said Shovel. "In a few months they will grow tall and bloom. We will have colorful, sweet-smelling flowers all over the garden!"

"It takes a few months for them to grow?" asked Blue.

"Sure," said Pail. "It takes time for plants to grow. Some take longer than others."

"When these bulbs finally grow into beautiful lilies," said Pail, "we will be glad we waited!"

Blue went inside and looked at her plant.

"You take your time, seedling. Just wait until you're ready," she told it quietly.

Blue checked the soil in the pot, added a bit of water, and placed it back in the sunlight. Then she headed outside to help Shovel and Pail plant their lily bulbs around the garden.

Blue continued to take care of her plant. She thought about how it needed to drink when it was thirsty, and how it used sunlight and air to make its own food. She noticed that it moved to follow the sun across the sky.

"Joe," she said, "I didn't realize it before, but my seedling is a very busy plant. It eats, drinks, gets exercise, and grows. . . . It does all of the things I do!"

One morning Blue saw that her seedling had finally grown two new leaves. She brought it to school.

"It's a sunflower!" she announced proudly.

SUNFLOWERS

Sunflower

That afternoon the students brought their pots outside, and Miss Marigold helped them replant their seedlings in the ground.

"What do plants need to grow big and strong?" asked Miss Marigold.

"Air, water, soil, and sunlight!" said Magenta.

"And one more thing," added Blue. "Time!"